DON'T WALK ALONE AT NIGHT!

Veronika Martenova Charles

Illustrated by David Parkins

Tundra Books

Text copyright © 2007 by Veronika Martenova Charles
Illustrations copyright © 2007 by David Parkins

Published in Canada by Tundra Books,
75 Sherbourne Street, Toronto, Ontario M5A 2P9

Published in the United States by Tundra Books of Northern New York,
P.O. Box 1030, Plattsburgh, New York 12901

Library of Congress Control Number: 2006925076

Library and Archives Canada Cataloguing in Publication

Charles, Veronika Martenova
    Don't walk alone at night! / Veronika Martenova Charles ; [illustrated by] David Parkins.

(Easy-to-read spooky tales)
ISBN 978–0–88776–782–1

    1. Horror tales, Canadian (English). 2. Children's stories, Canadian (English). I. Parkins, David II. Charles, Veronika Martenova. Easy-to-read spooky tales. III. Title.

PS8555.H42242D68 2007   jC813'.54   C2006–901941–X

ONTARIO ARTS COUNCIL
CONSEIL DES ARTS DE L'ONTARIO

We acknowledge the financial support of the Government of Canada through the Book Publishing Industry Development Program (BPIDP) and that of the Government of Ontario through the Ontario Media Development Corporation's Ontario Book Initiative. We further acknowledge the support of the Canada Council for the Arts and the Ontario Arts Council for our publishing program.

Printed and bound in Canada

2 3 4 5   14 13 12 11

CONTENTS

WALKING LEON HOME
PART I

On Sunday, Leon and Marcos

had come over to play.

Now it was getting dark.

We were sitting on the porch

waiting for Leon's mother.

"Leon," my father called,

"your mom is on the phone.

Her car won't start."

"Tell her not to worry.

I'll walk home," Leon said.

"Don't walk alone at night!"

my father told him.

"Marcos and I will go with him,"

I said. "Can we?"

"All right," my father said.

"But take a sweater.

It's getting chilly."

We started on our way.

"I wasn't scared to walk alone,"

Leon said.

"But you have to pass a graveyard.

Creepy things can happen there

if you walk alone at night.

You might see a ghost!" Marcos said.

"Ghosts can't hurt you," Leon said.

"They're just made of air."

"Maybe," said Marcos,

"but they *can* suck your blood."

"Ghosts don't do that," I said.

"Vampires do."

"What would you do if you saw

a ghost?" Marcos asked.

"I would try to trick him,

like the girl in a story I know,"

I answered.

"Tell us the story," said Leon.

★

EMMA AND THE GHOST

(My Story)

Emma was sleeping over

at her grandmother's house.

"Tomorrow we'll visit your

grandfather,"

Grandmother told Emma.

"But Grandfather is dead,"

said Emma.

"Yes, but it's nice to go

to the cemetery.

We'll take flowers for him,"

said Grandmother.

The next day they went

to the graveyard.

At the gate, Grandmother filled

a bucket with water.

"First, we have to clean the grave,"

she said.

"I'll help," said Emma.

Emma took off her gold ring

and put it on the tombstone.

They cleaned the grave

and left flowers in a vase.

Back at home,

Emma washed her hands

before dinner.

"Oh, no!" she cried.

"I left my ring at the cemetery!

I have to go back to get it."

"Don't walk alone at night!"

Grandmother told her.

"We'll go in the morning."

"It might be gone by then.

I have to go now!" said Emma.

"I'll take the flashlight."

The graveyard

looked different at night.

It was deserted

and full of shadows.

Emma walked in.

A cloud of mist

rose between the graves.

WHAT WAS THAT?

The cloud floated over to her

and changed into an ugly old man.

IT WAS A GHOST!

Emma was terrified,

but she made herself smile.

"Good evening!" she said.

"It's not good for *you*,

young lady," the man said.

"I'm a GHOST!"

"Yes . . . well so am I," said Emma.

"You are?" the ghost asked.

"But you don't *look* like one."

"That's because . . . because . . .

I just died this morning!

I'm a new ghost," Emma lied.

"But *you* look like a wise ghost.

I could learn from you."

"True," the ghost agreed.

"I can scare people to death."

"Tell me," said Emma,

"is there anything we ghosts

are afraid of?"

"Light," the ghost said.

Emma pulled out her flashlight

and aimed it at the ghost.

In the bright light,

he quickly faded away.

Emma ran, grabbed her ring,

and returned to Grandmother's house.

"I was worried about you,"

Grandmother said.

"Now I know why," Emma replied.

"I found my ring,

but I shouldn't have gone by myself."

★   ★   ★

"It's good Emma had the flashlight.

It saved her," said Leon.

"Would you ever visit a cemetery

at night?" Marcos asked.

"I might," I said.

"It's not that scary.

Big bugs are worse."

"Or monsters waiting in the dark," said Leon. "They can grab you when you're alone and stuff you in a bag."

"What do you mean?" I asked.

"I'll tell you a story," said Leon.

MONSTER

(Leon's Story)

Babu and his two sisters

were looking for pretty shells.

"Look at this one!" said Babu,

showing the shell to his sisters.

"It has the shape of a snake on it.

I'll keep it for good luck."

Babu hid the shell under a bush

so he could find it again.

"I'll get it on the way home,"

he said.

But Babu forgot about it

until they were almost home

that evening.

"Let's go back!" Babu said.

"No!" said his older sister.

"I've heard that a monster

goes walking there at night."

"But it's not night yet," Babu said.

"If you won't come, I'll go alone."

"Don't walk alone at night!"

his sisters told him.

"I'll be home in no time,"

Babu promised, and started off.

But he *was* a bit afraid,

so he sang to feel brave.

When he came to the bush,

a man was sitting there

beside a drum.

He had Babu's shell.

"You have a sweet voice,"

the man said to Babu.

"Why did you come here?"

"That shell in your hand is mine.

Please, may I have it?"

Babu asked.

"Of course," the man said.

"But first, sing some more!

I can't hear very well,

so come closer."

Suddenly, the man changed

into a monster with two heads.

He grabbed Babu

and stuffed him into his drum.

"LET ME OUT!" screamed Babu.

"No!" said the monster.

"You'll be the voice of my drum.

When I beat on it, you will sing

and people will give me food."

He picked up the drum

with Babu in it, and left.

In every village the monster

changed back into a man.

He played his drum and was paid

with chickens and yams.

Then he came to Babu's village.

Babu's sisters heard

the singing drum.

"Listen!" the sisters gasped.

"It's Babu's voice!"

Quickly, they ran and told

their mother and father.

Their parents invited

the man home for dinner.

They gave him food and drinks

until he fell asleep.

Babu's parents opened the drum,

freed Babu, and hid him.

Then they filled the drum

with spiders and bees,

and closed it up again.

"Wake up!"

the parents called to the man.

Our neighbors want to hear

your wonderful singing drum."

The man went outside

and began to beat his drum.

There was silence.

He pounded the drum again,

but it did not sing.

The man became angry.

He pulled the skin off the drum.

The bees escaped from inside

and stung him.

In his panic, the man changed

into the two-headed monster.

Then spiders bit him,

and the monster died.

When it was all over,

The parents said to Babu,

"Next time you go out,

stay with your sisters

and come home before dark!"

And Babu did.

38

"Was that scary?" Leon asked.

"Not very," I answered.

"But you told me

you don't like bugs," said Leon.

"I meant *big* bugs," I replied.

"I'll tell you a story about

a big bug," said Marcos.

★

THE MOTHMAN

(Marcos' Story)

"What are those? Candies?"

Max asked his mother.

She was putting little white balls

into the closet.

"They are mothballs.

Moths are eating our clothes,"

his mother said.

She pulled her sweater out of

the closet.

"Look! It's full of holes.

Can you please take it to Aunt Rose

and ask her to fix it?"

"All right," said Max.

It was getting dark when Max

arrived at his aunt's house.

Big brown moths sat

on her porch.

He gave his aunt the sweater.

"It's dark outside," Aunt Rose said.

"Don't walk alone at night!

I'll take you home."

"No need to," Max said.

"If you lend me your bike,

I'll bring it back tomorrow."

On a lonely stretch of the road

halfway back to his house,

Max saw a large figure.

It was bigger than a man

and it stared at him

with glowing red eyes.

As Max neared, it rose into the air

like a giant butterfly. A Mothman!

It swooped down toward him.

Max pedaled with all his strength.

The creature must be hungry,

thought Max.

He tossed his own sweater to it.

The Mothman landed on the road

and gobbled up the sweater.

Max turned into the lane

leading to his house.

It was dark among the trees.

The bike hit a stone

and Max fell to the ground.

He looked up into the trees.

The Mothman was gliding

through the branches,

down, down toward Max. . . .

★   ★   ★

WALKING LEON HOME
PART 2

"Watch out!" Marcos said.

"The Mothman could be up there!"

Big trees bent over the road.

We were coming to the graveyard.

"Would you *really* go in there

at night?" Leon asked.

"Sure! I'm not afraid.

Are you?" I said.

"I will go if you and Marcos go,"

said Leon.

"Let's do it!" Marcos said.

We climbed over the gate

and walked by the graves.

Then we turned around.

A dark figure was coming

toward us.

"GHOST!" Leon cried.

We ran. I dropped my sweater.

"You!" someone shouted.

"Stop right there!"

A light shone on our faces.

"Is this yours?" a man asked,

handing me back my sweater.

"What are you boys up to?"

"We . . . we are GHOSTS!" said Leon.

"Don't get smart with me,"

the man said.

"I'm the caretaker,

and if I catch you here again,

I'll call your parents!"

We walked the rest of the way

to Leon's house in silence.

"Come in," said Leon's mom.

"It's cold out.

I got the car started. I'll drive you back."

"Don't worry. I have a sweater," I said,

and I put it on.

There were holes in the sleeves!

I turned to Leon's mother.

"Maybe it *would* be better

if you drove us home."

And so Leon's mother did.

AFTERWORD

At the end of the Mothman story,

the giant insect-man glides toward Max.

Is that the end of Max? What happens?

You can invent any ending to the story

you want.

WHERE THE STORIES COME FROM

Conversations with ghosts appear in the stories of many cultures. *Emma and the Ghost* is placed in central Europe, where daily visits to cemeteries by older women are common.

The story, *Monster*, is based on part of a folktale told in Africa.

The Mothman was inspired by reported sightings of a giant insect in West Virginia during the mid-sixties.